Storybook Treasury of Strawberry Shortcake

GROSSET & DUNLAP
Published by the Penguin Group
Penguin Group (USA) Inc., 375 Hudson Street, New York, New York 10014, U.S.A.
Penguin Group (Canada), 10 Alcorn Avenue, Toronto, Ontario, Canada M4V 3B2
(a division of Pearson Penguin Canada Inc.)
Penguin Books Ltd, 80 Strand, London WC2R ORL, England
Penguin Ireland, 25 St Stephen's Green, Dublin 2, Ireland
(a division of Penguin Books Ltd)
Penguin Group (Australia), 250 Camberwell Road, Camberwell, Victoria 3124, Australia
(a division of Pearson Australia Group Pty Ltd)
Penguin Books India Pvt Ltd, 11 Community Centre, Panchsheel Park, New Delhi - 110 017, India
Penguin Group (NZ), Cnr Airborne and Rosedale Roads, Albany, Auckland 1310, New Zealand
(a division of Pearson New Zealand Ltd)
Penguin Books (South Africa) (Pty) Ltd, 24 Sturdee Avenue, Rosebank, Johannesburg 2196, South Africa

Penguin Books Ltd, Registered Offices:
80 Strand, London WC2R ORL, England

STRAWBERRY SHORTCAKE STORYBOOK TREASURY published in 2005 by Grosset & Dunlap.
MEET STRAWBERRY SHORTCAKE originally published in 2003 by Grosset & Dunlap.
STRAWBERRY SHORTCAKE AT THE BEACH originally published in 2003 by Grosset & Dunlap.
SPRING FOR STRAWBERRY SHORTCAKE originally published in 2004 by Grosset & Dunlap.
MEET BLUEBERRY MUFFIN originally published in 2004 by Grosset & Dunlap.
STRAWBERRY SHORTCAKE SLEEPS OVER originally published in 2004 by Grosset & Dunlap.
STRAWBERRY SHORTCAKE'S SEABERRY MYSTERY originally published in 2005 by Grosset & Dunlap.

ISBN 0-448-44303-1   10 9 8 7 6 5 4 3 2 1

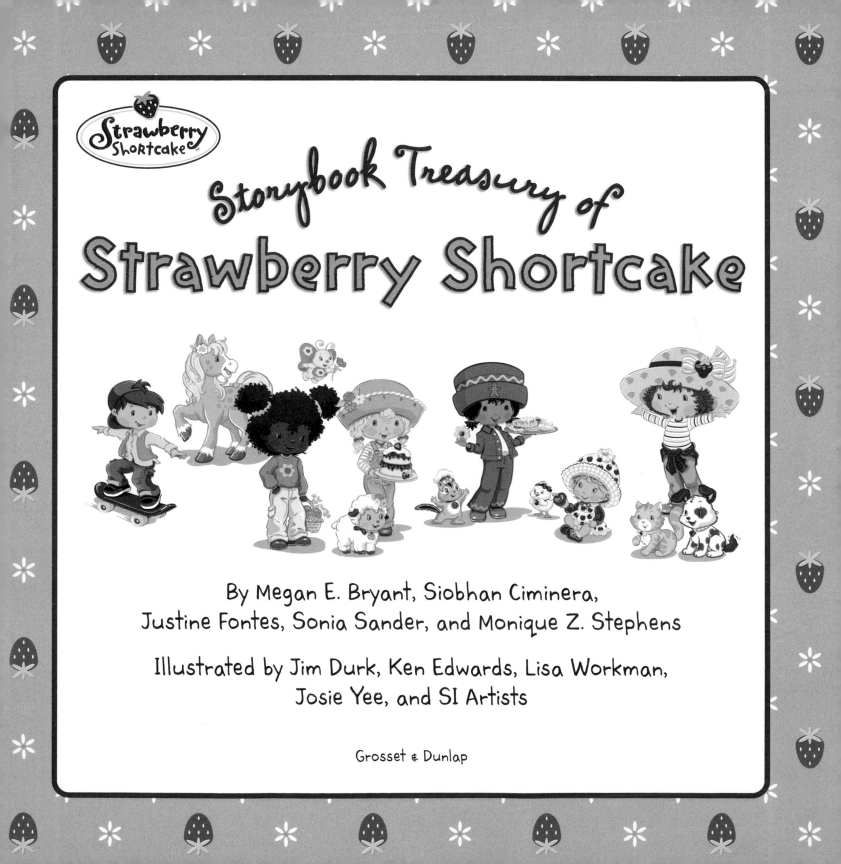

Storybook Treasury of
Strawberry Shortcake

By Megan E. Bryant, Siobhan Ciminera,
Justine Fontes, Sonia Sander, and Monique Z. Stephens

Illustrated by Jim Durk, Ken Edwards, Lisa Workman,
Josie Yee, and SI Artists

Grosset & Dunlap

Table of Contents

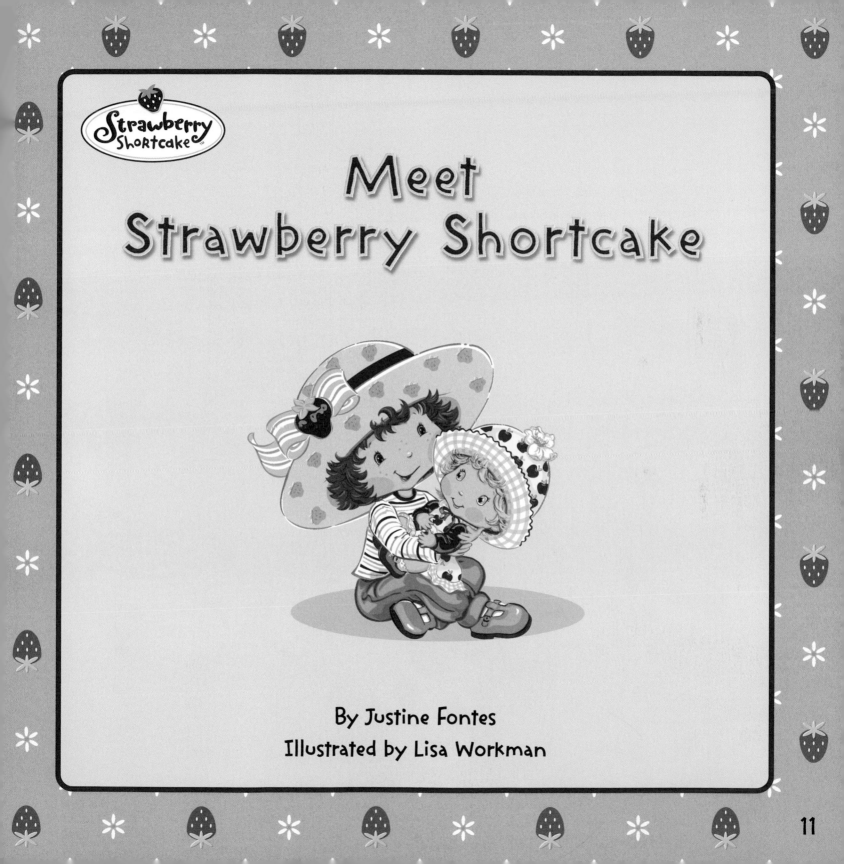

Meet
Strawberry Shortcake

By Justine Fontes

Illustrated by Lisa Workman

It was a special day in Strawberryland—Apple Dumplin's berry first birthday!

"Happy Birthday, Apple Dumplin'!" said Strawberry Shortcake. "To celebrate, we're going to have a party. But first we have some shopping to do!"

Strawberry made a list:
- COOKIES
- FRUIT
- JUICE
- PARTY HATS
- BIRTHDAY CAKE

Strawberry Shortcake brought her map.
"We have to take the Berry Trail," she said. "And it looks like we'll have to travel to some berry, berry interesting lands to find everything we need."

"Is there a place on your map where folks meow and purr?" asked Custard.

"We'll have more fun if we meet different kinds of people," Strawberry replied. "The world would be a berry, berry boring place if we were all alike!"

Before long, they reached a village that smelled like warm cookies!

"Yummy!" Apple cried.

"This must be Cookie Corners," said Strawberry Shortcake. "We should have a berry easy time finding cookies here!"

Just then, the door of a bakery opened and a girl rolled out a cart full of cookies. Pupcake was so excited, he ran right into her. Cookies flew everywhere!

"Oh macaroonio!" the girl exclaimed. She looked very upset.

"I'm sorry," Strawberry Shortcake said. "Pupcake gets really excited when he meets new people."

"Woof!" barked Pupcake. Then he licked the girl's face. She giggled. "That's okay. Hi, I'm Ginger Snap," she said.

Ginger Snap took them inside her bakery. There they saw the most amazing cookie-making machine! It even made a tuna macaroon for Custard.

"A tuna cookie? Now that's really different," Strawberry Shortcake said.

"Different, but delicious," the cat purred.

Soon the girls were loading the pink wagon with cookies. Strawberry Shortcake was berry, berry happy—not just to have cookies, but a new friend as well!

She waved good-bye to Ginger Snap, then looked at her map. "Now we need to find fruit and juice. Next stop, Orange Blossom Acres!"

In Orange Blossom Acres, they saw a girl picking
fruit in an orchard.

"Hi. I'm Strawberry Shortcake," Strawberry
told the girl. "And this is my sister, Apple Dumplin'."

"I'm Orange Blossom," the girl said.

Strawberry told Orange Blossom about the party.
"Please take as much juice as you want, and fruit, too.
I've got plenty!" Orange Blossom said with a laugh.
Strawberry Shortcake thanked her new friend,
and got back on the Berry Trail.

The next town was made of giant cakes.
"No wonder it's called Cakewalk!" Strawberry Shortcake
exclaimed. They walked into a store called Angel Cake's
Cake Shoppe.

"Hi, I'm Angel Cake," said the girl behind the counter.
"Can I help you?"

She showed them photos of all kinds of cakes.
Apple cooed when she saw a cake covered in apples.

"This is the one!" Strawberry said. "We'll need it by
this afternoon."

"That's impossible!" Angel said. "It's too much work
for one person."

"What if we all work together?" Strawberry Shortcake suggested. "If you get the recipe, I can help you gather the ingredients. I'll pour. Apple will mix. Custard can clean up—and Pupcake can nap!"

Finally, the cake was done. "This was hard work," Strawberry Shortcake said, "but because we worked together, it was actually fun!"

Custard licked the counter clean. "I wouldn't go *that* far."

"Only a special cat could help the way you have," Angel said.

Custard purred.

Their next stop was Upper Hat Rack. But after walking for a while, Strawberry Shortcake checked the map and sighed. "We're berry, berry lost."

Just then, a pony trotted up to them. "I, Honey Pie Pony, am an expert in giving directions. Have you tried north? Or south? Or east? What about west? Then there's northeast and..."

"Could you tell us the way to Upper Hat Rack?"
Strawberry Shortcake asked.

"One of my favorite places, like Upper Coat
Rack, but less crowded. I'll take you there!"
the chatty pony replied.

Soon they were even more lost, and in a dark, scary forest!
Suddenly, Pupcake barked and ran ahead.
"Pupcake, wait!" Strawberry cried. She ran after Pupcake.
But Pupcake tumbled through a leaf-covered door.
He landed right in the arms of a strange boy!

"Hello, who are you?" Strawberry Shortcake asked the boy.
"Huckleberry Pie's my name. But you can call me Huck,"
the boy said. "And this is my fort, in the heart of Huckleberry Briar,"
he added proudly.

Strawberry Shortcake looked around. "That's a berry fine
spyglass you have," she said.

"Want to take a peek?" Huck offered.

Strawberry looked through the glass. She saw a river
made of chocolate. Huck offered to take them there.

The friends made their way through the thick woods.
"I almost forgot!" Strawberry Shortcake exclaimed.
"We need to get to Upper Hat Rack for party hats!"
"Oh, that's miles from here," Huck said. "But how about this?" Huck quickly twisted vines and berries into beautiful little hats.

Finally they arrived at the River Fudge. Pupcake was so excited, he ran in circles, jumping on and off the wagon. One big jump knocked the handle right out of Strawberry Shortcake's hand. The wagon rolled toward the river—with Apple Dumplin' in it!

"Uh-oh!" Apple cried in alarm.

Strawberry leaped onto Honey's back. "Giddy up!" she shouted.

Custard scrambled up a tree, then dropped onto the pony's back, too.

Strawberry Shortcake pulled a vine from her party hat.
Just before the wagon could roll into the river, she looped the
vine around the handle and pulled with all her might. The wagon
teetered on the edge of the chocolate stream, then stopped!

Strawberry Shortcake ran over and scooped up Apple Dumplin'. The baby was safe, but the wagon kept rolling! The party supplies bounced right out. Then the empty wagon fell into the river and floated away.

"Well, Apple and the party supplies are safe.
But how will we get them home without the wagon?"
Strawberry Shortcake wondered.

"I know just the way," said Huck. He told them
his plan, and everyone got to work.

"There's nothing like a raft to get you across a river," Strawberry said. "And nothing like working together to get the job done."

"I never realized how much fun it was to work with others," Huck added.

"Me either," said Custard, surprised.

They loaded the raft and waved good-bye.

Back in Strawberryland, Strawberry Shortcake had everything she needed for the party—except guests! She quickly solved that problem by inviting all their new friends.

Huckleberry Pie, Honey Pie, Orange Blossom, Angel Cake, and Ginger Snap all came to wish Apple Dumplin' "A Berry Happy Birthday."

Everyone had a wonderful time, even Custard. Not one of their new friends had whiskers, but that didn't matter.

"Parties really are more fun when you have all different kinds of guests," the cat admitted.

Strawberry Shortcake laughed. "Custard, I couldn't agree more!"

Strawberry Shortcake at the Beach

By Megan E. Bryant

Illustrated by SI Artists

One bright, sunny morning, Strawberry Shortcake woke up and looked out the window. "It's a berry perfect beach day!" she exclaimed. "Wake up, Apple Dumplin'!"

"Beach?" asked Apple Dumplin' sleepily.

"That's right! We're going to Seaberry Beach today with all of our friends," Strawberry said.

They quickly packed everything they would need: two fluffy towels, sunblock, a yummy picnic lunch, and all of their beach toys.

"I can't forget these!" Strawberry Shortcake told Apple. "My new sunglasses!" She put them on, and they were ready to go.

"Hi, Strawberry!" Huck called as Strawberry walked up to her friends at their meeting place.

"Hi, everybody," Strawberry said.

"Wow! Those sunglasses are great, Strawberry!" Angel Cake said. "Can I try them on?"

"Sure," Strawberry Shortcake replied. "You can borrow them for the day if you want. Just be berry careful with them, please."

"I will," promised Angel. "Thanks!"

Soon the kids arrived at Seaberry Beach. They went straight to their favorite spot near the lifeguard station and laid out their beach towels.

"Hold still, Apple," said Strawberry Shortcake. Her little sister giggled and squirmed while Strawberry put sunblock on her.

"Let's play catch!" Huck said, getting out his beach ball. The friends made a large circle and played ball.

"It's too hot to play ball anymore," Strawberry Shortcake said to her friends. "Who wants to go in the water?" she asked.

"Me!" shouted everybody at once.

"Don't forget to stay with your buddy," Strawberry reminded her friends. Holding hands, they all raced down to the ocean. The friends laughed and splashed as they played in the water.

"The waves are getting bigger," Strawberry Shortcake said to Orange Blossom. "Do you think that Angel and Ginger are too far out?"

"Maybe," Orange said. She looked a little worried.

"Hey, Ginger! Angel!" Huck yelled. But the waves were crashing so loudly that the girls could barely hear him. Angel turned around to wave to her friends.

Suddenly, a big wave knocked her down!

Angel slowly sat up, wiping the salty water out of her eyes.

"Angel! Angel!" her friends called as they ran over to her. They helped her to her feet.

"Did you get hurt?" Strawberry asked.

"No, I'm okay," said Angel Cake.

"Whoa, Angel, that wave was huge!" Huck said. "You have to be careful not to turn your back on the ocean when you play in the water!"

"I think she knows that now," said Strawberry Shortcake with a smile as she took a piece of seaweed off of Angel's hat.

"Well, let's go have our picnic!" said Orange Blossom. "I'm really hungry!"
Suddenly, Angel Cake felt something snap beneath her foot. She looked down, and her hands flew to her face.

Oh, no! she thought. *I broke Strawberry's sunglasses!*

Angel Cake held the broken glasses tightly as she trudged up the sand after her friends.

"Would you like some of these sweet, juicy strawberries from my garden?" Strawberry Shortcake asked. "They're berry delicious!"

I can't tell Strawberry about her sunglasses now, Angel thought miserably. *It will ruin her whole day.*

"No thanks, I'm not very hungry," Angel said, trying to smile. As soon as she got a chance, Angel hid the sunglasses in her bag. *I'll tell Strawberry later,* Angel promised herself.

After the picnic, the friends built sand castles and played tag. Finally, it was time to go home.

"Bye, everybody!" Strawberry said to her friends. Then she turned to Angel. "Can I have my sunglasses back, please?"

Angel opened her mouth to tell Strawberry that the glasses were broken, but the words wouldn't come out. Instead she said, "Um, can I give them back tomorrow?"

"Sure," Strawberry said with a smile. "See you then!"

At home, Angel felt worse and worse about the broken sunglasses. She stroked her pet lamb's fleecy wool.

"Why didn't I just tell Strawberry that I broke her sunglasses?" she said to Vanilla Icing. "Now I've only made things worse! What if she won't be my friend anymore?"

Angel Cake sighed. "I don't know what to do. Maybe I should ask Ginger Snap for advice. She's good at fixing things."

"Hi, Angel Cake. Come in," said Ginger Snap. "What are you doing here?"

"I have a problem," said Angel sadly. She showed Ginger the broken sunglasses and explained what had happened. "I shouldn't have worn them in the water. Strawberry asked me to be careful! I'm afraid she'll be really mad."

"That is a tough problem," Ginger said. "But Angel, it was an accident. Just tell her you're sorry. I'm sure she'll understand. And if you go tell her now, you won't have to worry about it anymore. I can come with you if you want."

"Yes, please," said Angel. She wasn't looking forward to telling Strawberry, but already she felt a little better.

A few minutes later, Angel and Ginger knocked on Strawberry's front door.

"Hello!" said Strawberry Shortcake. "This is a berry nice surprise!"

"Strawberry, I have something to tell you," Angel Cake said in a soft voice. She took a deep breath and pulled the broken sunglasses out of her pocket. "When that big wave knocked me down at the beach, your sunglasses fell off my face. Then I stepped on them by accident and they broke. I'm really, really sorry. And I'm also sorry that I didn't tell you when it happened. Are you mad at me?"

"No, I'm not mad at you," Strawberry said to Angel Cake. "I know you didn't mean to break the sunglasses. It's okay."

"Really?" asked Angel

"Of course!" Strawberry replied. "The important thing is that you didn't get hurt when the wave knocked you down. That matters a lot more than the sunglasses!" Strawberry gave Angel a big hug.

Strawberry Shortcake looked at the sunglasses. "It's too bad they broke, though," she said. "They were my berry favorite sunglasses. Oh, well— I guess I'll just throw them away."

"Wait a minute," said Ginger Snap. "I have an idea!" She reached into her toolbox and pulled out a tube of glue. Ginger picked up the broken sunglasses. "A drop of glue here, a drop of glue there . . . good as new!"

"Oh, Ginger, thank you berry much for fixing my sunglasses!" Strawberry said.

"Thank you for fixing everything!" Angel Cake said to Ginger.

"You're welcome!" Ginger said. "I love to fix things for my friends!"

Strawberry Shortcake

Spring for Strawberry Shortcake

By Monique Z. Stephens

Illustrated by Josie Yee and Ken Edwards

It was a special day in Strawberryland—
planting day! Strawberry Shortcake had
been looking forward to this day for weeks.

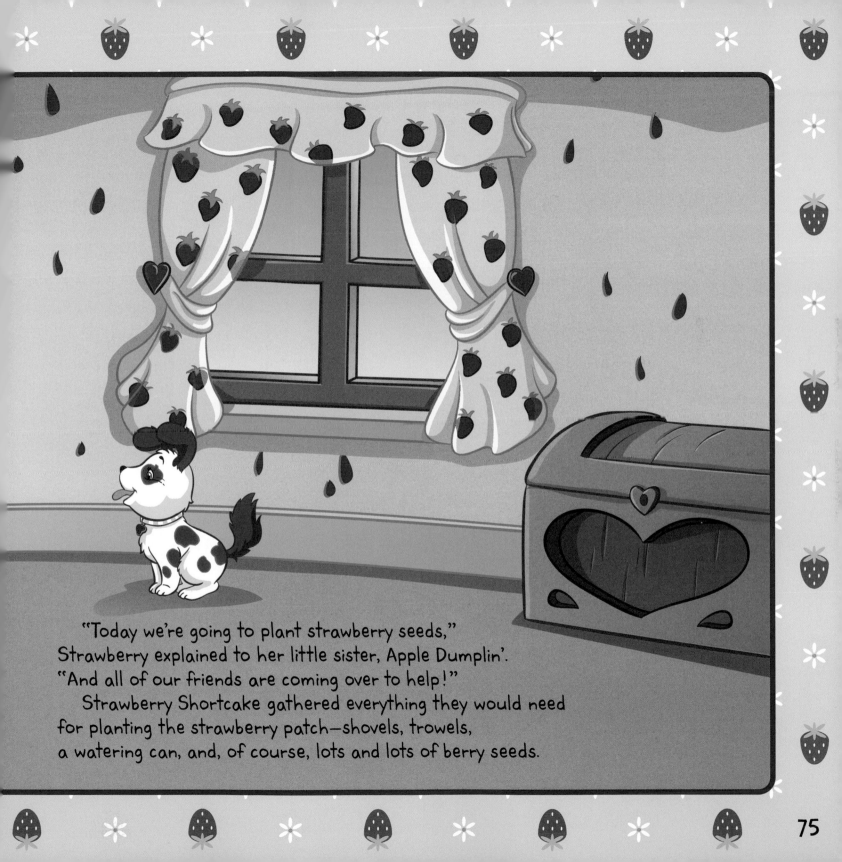

"Today we're going to plant strawberry seeds,"
Strawberry explained to her little sister, Apple Dumplin'.
"And all of our friends are coming over to help!"
Strawberry Shortcake gathered everything they would need
for planting the strawberry patch—shovels, trowels,
a watering can, and, of course, lots and lots of berry seeds.

There was a knock at the door. Strawberry smiled when she saw her friends Angel Cake, Huckleberry Pie, Orange Blossom, Ginger Snap, and Honey Pie Pony standing outside.

"Hi, Strawberry!" said Huck. "Are you ready to plant?"

Strawberry Shortcake shivered as an icy gust of wind blew through the doorway. Even the icicles hanging from the roof seemed to shiver! *"Brr!"* she exclaimed. "It's still berry cold, but we can get a head start on our planting if we work together!"

"Let's work in pairs," Strawberry suggested. "Huck and Custard can dig rows in the berry patch. Honey and Orange can scatter seeds in the rows. Angel and Ginger can water the seeds. And Apple and I will cover them back up!"

Pupcake barked.

Strawberry Shortcake laughed. "Don't worry, Pupcake, I didn't forget you. You can . . . supervise!"

She turned to her friends. "All right, everybody," said Strawberry. "Let's get started!"

Huck tried to put his shovel into the ground.
"Uh-oh!" said Huck. "I don't think we're going
to do much planting today. The ground
is too frozen to dig up!"

"Let me try," said Ginger Snap helpfully, picking up a shovel. But Ginger couldn't turn the soil either.

"That's strange," said Strawberry. "We always plant the berry seeds by now!"

"Spring must be late this year," Angel Cake said.

Strawberry Shortcake frowned. "I think you're right. But if spring is late, our planting will be late, and then we'll have fewer berries in the summer! We've got to find spring. Who wants to come with me?"

"I will!" Orange Blossom said quickly.

"So will I," volunteered Ginger Snap.

"And Angel Cake, Huckleberry, and I can stay here with Apple Dumplin', Custard, and Pupcake," Honey Pie Pony offered.

"That way, if spring arrives while you're gone, we can get right to work— so we don't lose any planting time!" added Angel Cake.

Strawberry Shortcake smiled gratefully. "Thanks, guys. Hopefully, we'll be back soon—and bring warmer weather with us!"

Waving good-bye, Strawberry, Orange, and Ginger set off to find spring.

The friends searched all of Strawberryland, looking for signs of spring. Suddenly, something caught Strawberry Shortcake's eye.

"Look! A daffodil!" she exclaimed. "It's a clue!"

"What do you mean?" asked Orange.

"Daffodils only bloom in springtime, so spring can't be too far away," Strawberry explained. "Look, there's another one! I bet spring is almost here!"

"That's a relief," said Ginger. "If spring doesn't come soon, Cookie Corners will run out of ingredients before summer!"

"Why would Cookie Corners run out of ingredients?" asked Strawberry, confused.

"Spring brings warm weather to grow fresh grain. The hens need grain to eat, so they can lay eggs," Ginger said. "And spring's warm sunshine makes the grass grow. Cows eat the grass to make milk and butter.

"And every spring, the farmers plant wheat and sugarcane, which give us flour and sugar," Ginger continued. "I need all of these things—eggs, milk, butter, flour, and sugar—to make cookies!"

"Spring is just as important in Orange Blossom Acres," said Orange. "Without spring, the bees and butterflies can't help the plants and flowers grow. That means that nothing will bloom in Orange Blossom Acres. And that means no fruit!"

"So it's a good thing spring is nearby," said Strawberry, pointing to a butterfly's cocoon.

"Right," said Orange. "But where is it?"

The girls continued their search through Huckleberry Briar to the frozen River Fudge. As they walked carefully along the icy bank, they met a frail-looking old man.

"Hello, sir," said Strawberry. "I'm Strawberry Shortcake, and these are my friends, Orange Blossom and Ginger Snap. Do you need any help?"

The old man smiled wearily. "I'm Old Man Winter. Thank you, but I'm fine. Just tired."

Strawberry, Orange, and Ginger nodded sympathetically. "We understand," said Strawberry Shortcake. "We're a little tired, too. We've been searching all over for spring. It should be here by now!"

"Yes," Old Man Winter agreed. "She *is* very late."

"*She?*" said Orange Blossom. "Spring is a *girl?*"

Old Man Winter nodded. "Yes, and she's not much older than you. She brings warm breezes, bright sunshine, and gentle showers to all the lands.

"But I don't think she wants to do her job this year. I've finished my work, but I can't go home until Spring comes," Old Man Winter said with a sigh.

"That's not fair!" said Strawberry Shortcake.

"No, it isn't," Old Man Winter replied sadly.

"Do you know where we can find her?" asked Ginger Snap.

"Go to the Land of Seasons," said Old Man Winter. "I expect she'll be there."

Strawberry, Orange, and Ginger thanked him and went on their way.

Strawberry Shortcake and her friends walked a long time before they finally arrived at the Land of Seasons. There, they found a little girl playing in the snow.

"Come play!" she called to them. "Come make snow angels with me!"

The girl looked like she was having so much fun that Strawberry, Orange, and Ginger couldn't resist joining her! The four girls laughed as they jumped and played in the snow.

Finally Strawberry stood up. "I wish we could keep playing, but we have an important job to do," she explained to the girl.

"But we're having so much fun!" the little girl complained.

"We've got to look for Spring," said Strawberry Shortcake. "If Spring doesn't come, I can't grow my beautiful berries."

"And I can't bake my yummy-licious cookies," said Ginger Snap.

"And I won't have any fruit to make the world's juiciest juice!" Orange Blossom added.
"Don't forget Old Man Winter," Strawberry reminded her friends. "He can't even go home!"

The little girl looked at the ground. "I didn't know Spring was so important," she said in a soft voice.

"Important?" Strawberry exclaimed. "Everyone's counting on her!"

Slowly, the girl took off her scarf and mittens. "Maybe I can help," she said. "You see . . . I'm Spring."

The girls stared at her with their mouths open. "You're Spring?" they said together.

Spring nodded. "That's right. And I think we'd better get going. I have a job to do!"

Strawberry, Orange, and Ginger ran after Spring as she danced from place to place, bringing springtime to all the different lands with her special wand.

Like magic, the sun shone more brightly, the wind blew more gently, and the hard ground thawed. Bare trees sprouted leaves, flowers bloomed, and butterflies emerged from their cocoons.

Spring had arrived!

When they reached Strawberry's house in Strawberryland, Honey, Huck, and Angel had already started planting.

"Thanks for working so berry hard, everybody," Strawberry Shortcake said. Then she turned to her new friend. "Spring, you're wonderful!" she said. "We're so glad you came back!"

"Thank you," said Spring. "And thank you for reminding me how important it is to do my part when there's work to be done!"

"Speaking of work—there's lots of planting to do. So we'd better get busy!" said Strawberry Shortcake.

"We can even make it a planting party," said Orange Blossom. "I brought juice!"

"And I brought cookies!" Ginger said.

"Good idea," said Strawberry Shortcake. "After all, work can be fun . . ."

" . . . when we all do our part!" Spring finished with a big smile as she picked up a shovel.

Strawberry Shortcake laughed happily. "And soon we'll have the berry best strawberry crop ever!"

Meet Blueberry Muffin

By Sonia Sander

Illustrated by SI Artists

Blueberry Muffin had just moved to Blueberry Valley, but she already felt at home—thanks to Strawberry Shortcake and her pals.

"We're really lucky to have made lots of new friends!" Blueberry Muffin said to her pet mouse, Cheesecake. "How can I thank them for making me feel so welcome?"

Suddenly, Cheesecake dashed into the house. He quickly
returned wearing a party hat from Blueberry Muffin's
collection of dress-up clothes. Blueberry Muffin burst
out laughing as Cheesecake did a funny little dance.

"Great idea! We can have a party—a berry fun housewarming
party!" Blueberry Muffin exclaimed. "I can't wait to invite all of
our new friends!"

Blueberry Muffin made invitations for the party, then set off down the Berry Trail to deliver them. Her first stop was Strawberry Shortcake's house, where Orange Blossom was helping Strawberry in her garden.

"Hi, Strawberry Shortcake! Hi, Orange Blossom!" Blueberry Muffin said as she gave them their invitations. "I'm having a party at my house tomorrow. I hope you can come."

"I'd love to!" replied Strawberry Shortcake. "Thanks for inviting us."

"It sounds berry fun!" added Orange.

"Can we do anything to help?" Strawberry asked.

Blueberry Muffin shook her head. "No, no, this party is my way of thanking you for being such nice friends!"

"I'm so glad Blueberry Muffin moved here," Strawberry said.

"Me, too," agreed Orange Blossom. "I want to make a berry special present for her! I'd better go home so I can get started right away."

"But we're supposed to go to Ginger Snap's house this afternoon," Strawberry Shortcake reminded Orange.

"I'm sure Ginger will understand," Orange Blossom said. "After all, she has to get ready for Blueberry's party, too. Let's call her."

"Hi, Ginger Snap, it's Orange Blossom."

"Hi! Guess what? Blueberry Muffin is having a party tomorrow!" Ginger Snap said excitedly.

"I know," Orange replied. "Strawberry and I have to get ready, so we can't come over today. I'm sorry."

"Oh, okay," Ginger Snap said. "Well, I guess I'll see you tomorrow. Bye."

I was really looking forward to my friends coming over, Ginger Snap thought sadly. *Oh, well. I guess we can have a tea party another time.*

The next day, all of the kids went to Blueberry Muffin's house for the party.

"Hi, everybody!" Blueberry Muffin called from her doorway. "I'm so glad you could come to my party!"

I wish Strawberry Shortcake and Orange Blossom had come to my party yesterday, Ginger Snap thought. But I guess they thought Blueberry Muffin's party was more important than mine.

"Blueberry Muffin, your house looks berry beautiful!"
Strawberry Shortcake exclaimed.

"And something sure smells delicious," added Huckleberry Pie.

"I made a fresh batch of my blueberry muffins," Blueberry
said. "Help yourself! There's plenty for everyone."

"I brought you some cookies," Ginger Snap said shyly to
Blueberry Muffin.

"Thank you!" Blueberry Muffin replied. "I love cookies!"

"I love these muffins!" Huck exclaimed as he took a big bite of his muffin.

"Can I have your recipe, Blueberry Muffin?" asked Strawberry.

"Of course!" Blueberry Muffin said.

No one is saying nice things about my cookies, Ginger Snap thought as she ate her muffin. *They must like the muffins better.*

"Don't forget to open your presents," Angel Cake told Blueberry after the kids finished their muffins.

"Yes, open mine first, please," said Strawberry Shortcake.

"Open mine next!" Huck said.

"Sit next to me, Blueberry!" Angel exclaimed.

Look at all those presents, Ginger Snap thought. Blueberry Muffin is really lucky!

"Thank you so much for the wonderful presents, everybody!" Blueberry Muffin said after she had opened all of her gifts. "Now who's ready for a game of musical chairs?"

Ginger Snap watched as all of her friends scrambled to get a spot next to Blueberry Muffin— even Strawberry Shortcake.

Strawberry Shortcake always stands next to me when we play musical chairs! Ginger Snap thought. But now she only wants to be with Blueberry Muffin—just like everybody else. I bet no one would even notice if I wasn't here.

"I'm going to go home now," Ginger Snap said in a quiet voice. But the other kids were laughing so loudly that no one heard her.

Outside, Ginger Snap sadly watched all of her friends having a wonderful time at the party—without her. They don't miss me at all, Ginger Snap thought sadly. All they care about is being friends with Blueberry Muffin. I wish she had never moved here!

The next day, Ginger Snap still felt sad. She was baking a batch of cookies to cheer herself up when the phone rang.

"Hello?"

"Hi, Ginger, it's Blueberry Muffin. Everybody's coming over to go blueberry picking today. Would you like to come, too?"

"No, I can't," Ginger said. *I don't want to spend another day watching Blueberry Muffin take away my friends!*

"Oh," Blueberry said sadly. "Okay. Bye."

Ginger Snap started to feel guilty as soon as she hung up. *I wasn't very polite to Blueberry Muffin on the phone,* she thought. *And I shouldn't have left her party early, either.* As Ginger Snap sat alone in her cookie cottage, she couldn't stop thinking about her friends having a great time berry picking— and how rude she'd been to Blueberry Muffin.

"Oh, macaroonio!" Ginger Snap sighed. "Why would anyone want to be my friend after the way I've acted? I wish I could take it all back and start over."

Just then, there was a knock at the door. It was Strawberry Shortcake.

"Hi, Ginger Snap," she said. "Is everything okay? We were berry worried when you left the party early yesterday and didn't come berry picking today—especially Blueberry Muffin. She thought some muffins might make you feel better. And there's a note, too."

Dear Ginger Snap,
I'm sorry that you couldn't come berry picking today. It won't be as much fun without you. I hope you can come over another time. And I hope you like these muffins — they're my favorite!
♡ Love,
Blueberry Muffin

Suddenly, Ginger Snap began to cry. "I haven't been very nice, Strawberry," she said. "I thought everyone liked Blueberry Muffin more than me. I started to wish that she had never moved here."

"Oh, Ginger Snap!" Strawberry Shortcake exclaimed. "Everyone was just trying to make Blueberry Muffin feel welcome. We could never stop liking you. Old friends are just as important as new friends—and you'll always be one of my berry best friends!"

"Really?" Ginger Snap asked, wiping her eyes.

"Of course! Come on, let's go blueberry picking. All of our friends are waiting for us!"

Strawberry Shortcake and Ginger Snap hurried over to Blueberry Muffin's house.

"Look! Strawberry Shortcake's back—and she's brought Ginger Snap!" Blueberry Muffin exclaimed. "Hooray!"

"Hi, Ginger! I was just telling Blueberry all about your cool inventions," Huck said.

"And the way you can fix just about anything," added Orange Blossom.

"Come pick some blueberries with me!" called Angel Cake.

Ginger Snap grinned at her friends. "I will!" she said. "But there's something berry important I have to do first."

Ginger Snap turned to Blueberry Muffin. "I haven't been a very good friend," she said quietly. "I'm sorry for leaving your party early and for being rude to you on the phone. I'd really like to be friends with you. Would you give me another chance?"

Blueberry Muffin gave Ginger Snap a berry big hug. "How about we forget everything and start over?" Blueberry Muffin asked.

Ginger Snap wasn't quite sure what Blueberry Muffin meant—but she didn't have to wait long to find out.

"Hi, my name's Blueberry Muffin," said Blueberry Muffin, reaching out to shake Ginger Snap's hand. "I just moved here and I don't know anyone."

"My name's Ginger Snap. I'd be happy to show you around and introduce you to my friends," replied Ginger Snap with a smile. "Here in Strawberryland, there's always room for new friends!"

Strawberry Shortcake Sleeps Over

By Siobhan Ciminera

Illustrated by SI Artists

Orange Blossom was berry excited—it was the night of her big sleepover party! She had been planning it for weeks.

"Let's see," Orange Blossom said to her pet butterfly, Marmalade, as she checked her list. "We cleaned the house and made the food. We planned all of the activities for the party. Now all that's left is decorating!"

Just then, the doorbell rang. It was Strawberry Shortcake.

"Hi, Strawberry!" Orange Blossom said, looking at the clock. "You're early! The party doesn't start for another hour."

"I'm sorry, Orange," Strawberry said. "I was so excited about your party, I just couldn't wait."

"That's okay," said Orange. "Would you like to help me put up the decorations?"

"Sure!" replied Strawberry. "Look at all these pretty balloons and streamers!"

At five o'clock, Angel Cake and Ginger Snap arrived, right on time. "Yay! Everybody's here! Now the party can start!" Orange Blossom said excitedly. "Would you like some fresh-squeezed orange juice? I made it myself!"

"*Mmm, this is delicious!*" exclaimed Strawberry Shortcake after her first sip of juice.

"Thanks," said Orange Blossom, smiling. "I want everything to be perfect for my sleepover party! I've planned the whole night."

"Let's make some pictures now," Orange Blossom said, checking her list after the girls finished their juice. "I have crayons and markers and lots of pretty paper. I also have ribbons and sequins and magazine cut-outs if you want to make collages."

"That sounds fun!" said Ginger Snap. "I want to make a collage of my cookie factory."

"And I want to make a collage of the *beautiful* cake I made the other day," Angel Cake replied.

"I'm going to draw pictures of my pets, Custard and Pupcake!" exclaimed Strawberry Shortcake.

"Berry cool!" said Orange Blossom.

"And I'll draw a picture of us at the sleepover party! Let's do it!"

As everyone admired the pictures and collages, Orange Blossom checked her list. "Now it's time for dinner," she said. "We're going to have mini-pizzas! I have lots of toppings, so we can each make our own."

"I love pizza!" Ginger Snap exclaimed.
"Me, too," said Strawberry Shortcake.
"Mini-pizzas are fun to make and fun to eat!"

After dinner, Orange Blossom checked her list again. "Story time!" she said.

"It's too early for a story," replied Angel Cake. "Let's make friendship bracelets instead! I brought some pretty string and sparkly beads."

Orange shook her head. "No, it's story time now, and then we'll play a game, and then we'll go to bed."

Angel Cake frowned. "But I think..."

"No!" Orange interrupted. "This is my sleepover and I want to read a story!"

"Fine," said Angel. "Then I'm going home." She stormed out of Orange Blossom's tree house, slamming the door behind her.

Orange Blossom sat down and started to cry. "I just wanted to have a fun sleepover party for my friends!" she sobbed. "Now Angel Cake is mad at me!"

Strawberry Shortcake put her arm around Orange.

"Don't cry, Orange," Strawberry said kindly. "Angel's not mad at you—her feelings were hurt because she thought you didn't like her idea. But parties can be even more fun when friends take turns doing their favorite things."

Orange Blossom thought for a moment. "You're right, Strawberry," she finally said. "I didn't mean to be so bossy. I wish Angel Cake was still here so I could tell her that myself."

Then Orange Blossom had an idea. "I know!" she exclaimed. "I can go to Angel's house right now and tell her I'm sorry!"

"Berry good idea!" said Strawberry Shortcake. "Let's all go!"

"And we can bring her back to the party," added Ginger Snap.

Strawberry, Ginger, and Orange grabbed flashlights and jackets. Before they walked outside, Orange Blossom turned to her friends and said, "I feel so much better now. Thanks!"

A full moon brightened the night sky, and the girls didn't need their flashlights to find their way to Angel Cake's house.

"Let's play flashlight tag!" Ginger Snap suggested on the way to Cakewalk.

"Berry cool," replied Strawberry Shortcake. "Not it!"

"Not it!" returned Ginger. "Looks like you'll have to come get us, Orange!"

The girls giggled as they raced down the Berry Trail.

A few minutes later, the friends arrived at Angel Cake's house. Orange Blossom shyly knocked on the door.

Angel Cake looked surprised to see her. "Hi," she said quietly.

"Hi, Angel," replied Orange. She took a deep breath. "Angel, I'm so sorry I was bossy at my party. I didn't mean to hurt your feelings."

"Thanks, Orange," said Angel with a smile. "I'm sorry, too. I feel so silly for getting mad and running out of your party. Can we start over?"

"Absolutely!" exclaimed Orange Blossom, giving her friend a hug.

On the way to her tree house, Orange Blossom turned to Angel Cake and said, "When we get back, let's make some friendship bracelets."

154

"Or we could listen to a story," Angel quickly replied.

"Wait a minute," Strawberry Shortcake interrupted. "Let's make friendship bracelets and listen to a story at the same time!"

"Berry good idea," said Ginger Snap. "Let's race! On your mark, get set, go!"

When the girls returned to Orange Blossom Acres, they changed into their pajamas and took turns telling funny stories. The four friends laughed and laughed while they made pretty friendship bracelets.

After she finished telling her story, Orange Blossom turned to Angel Cake and handed her a beautiful friendship bracelet with pink and purple beads. "I made this for you, Angel," Orange said. "I'm so glad we're friends, and that you came to my sleepover party!"

"And I made this for you!" Angel Cake handed Orange Blossom a bracelet with red and orange beads. "I'm glad we're friends, too. Thanks for having such a great party!"

"I think it's time to go to bed now," Orange Blossom said with a yawn. "Look, Ginger Snap is already asleep!"

The girls giggled quietly.

"I'm tired, too," whispered Angel Cake. "Good night, everybody! I had a great time."

"So did I!" added Strawberry Shortcake as she turned out the light. "Berry sweet dreams, Angel and Orange!"

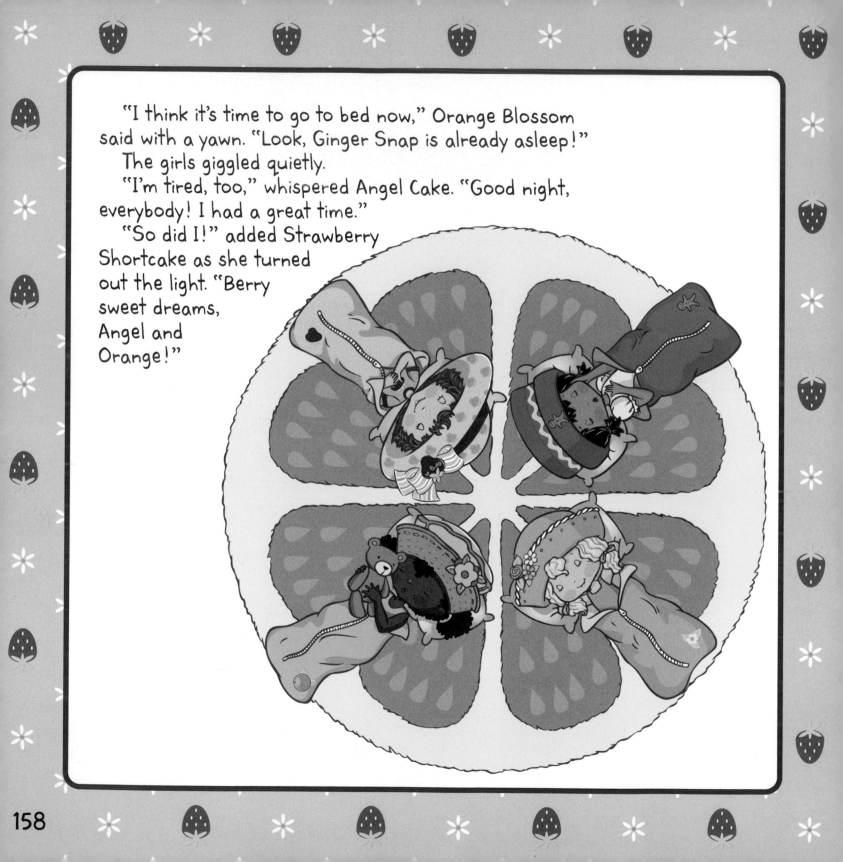

Strawberry Shortcake's Seaberry Mystery

By Sonia Sander

Illustrated by Josie Yee and Jim Durk

Strawberry Shortcake was busy working in her berry patch when her friend Coco Calypso's pet parrot swooped in for a landing. "Hello, Papaya Parrot!" called Strawberry Shortcake. "What brings you all the way to Strawberryland?"

"It's Coco! Oh, poor kid! Awful—dreadful—terrible—don't know where to start!" squawked Papaya Parrot.

"Whoa, Papaya, slow down! Here, have some strawberry punch and start over," Strawberry suggested.

"Someone's stealing all of Coco's seaberries, and she can't make her world-famous seaberry treats! We don't know why or who or when or how, but we need your help, Strawberry!" pleaded Papaya Parrot.

"Of course I'll help!" said Strawberry Shortcake. "Let's go! Seaberry Beach is berry far away, but I know a friend who can help us get there in no time."

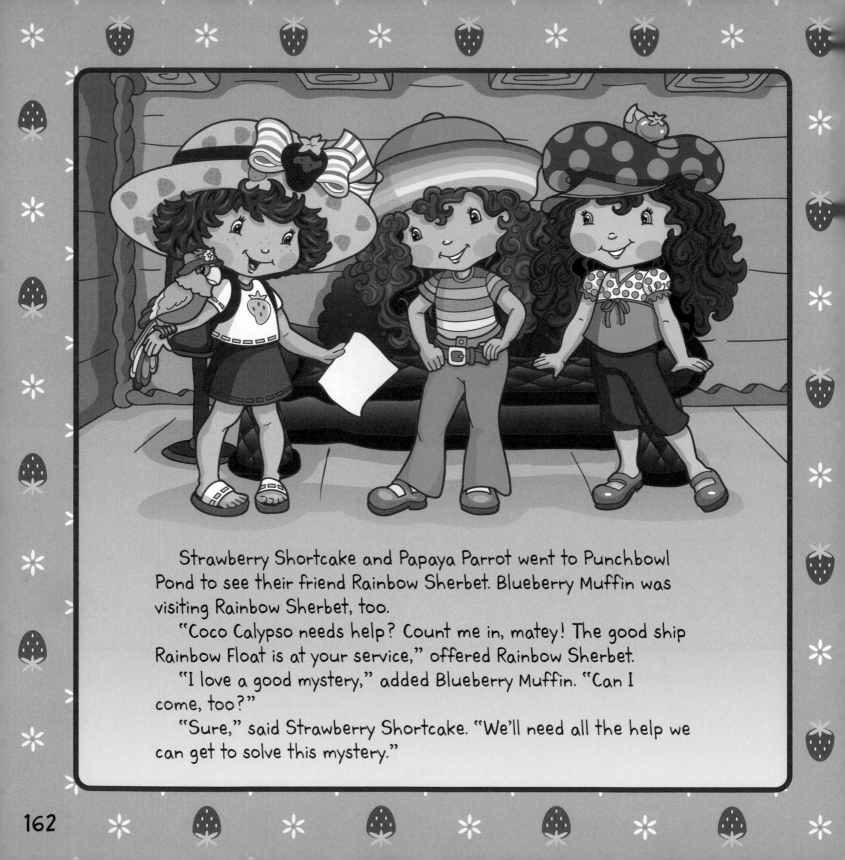

Strawberry Shortcake and Papaya Parrot went to Punchbowl Pond to see their friend Rainbow Sherbet. Blueberry Muffin was visiting Rainbow Sherbet, too.

"Coco Calypso needs help? Count me in, matey! The good ship Rainbow Float is at your service," offered Rainbow Sherbet.

"I love a good mystery," added Blueberry Muffin. "Can I come, too?"

"Sure," said Strawberry Shortcake. "We'll need all the help we can get to solve this mystery."

Rainbow Sherbet steered her houseboat out of Punchbowl Pond.

"The Soda Stream will take us right to Seaberry Beach," Strawberry Shortcake said, checking her map. "As long as we sail straight ahead, we can't get lost!"

With Strawberry's directions and Rainbow's steering, the three friends reached Seaberry Beach in a few hours. They changed into their summer clothes and set off for shore.

"We're here! We're home! We're home sweet home!" Papaya Parrot squawked happily.

"Hello, everybody!" called Coco Calypso from shore. "Welcome to Seaberry Beach!"

As soon as Strawberry and her friends were ashore, Coco told them about the stolen seaberries.

"It all started a few weeks ago. I gathered seaberries and left them on the beach, like I do every day. But the next morning, the seaberries were gone! All that was left was a trail of them leading into the lagoon. Now this happens every single night!"

Strawberry gave Coco Calypso a berry big hug. "Don't worry, Coco. Now that we're here, we'll make sure that it doesn't happen again—even if we have to stay up all night! Right, girls?"

"That's right!" Blueberry Muffin exclaimed. "You can count on us."

"Abso-berry-lutely!" added Rainbow Sherbet.

"Here's the plan—we'll watch . . ." began Strawberry Shortcake. She stopped and looked at the lagoon. "I have the strangest feeling that *we're* being watched right now."

"What was *that*?" Blueberry Muffin asked, pointing to the sea. The four friends glimpsed something shiny slip silently into the water.

"It was probably just a fish," Coco said. "Come on! It's almost dinnertime."

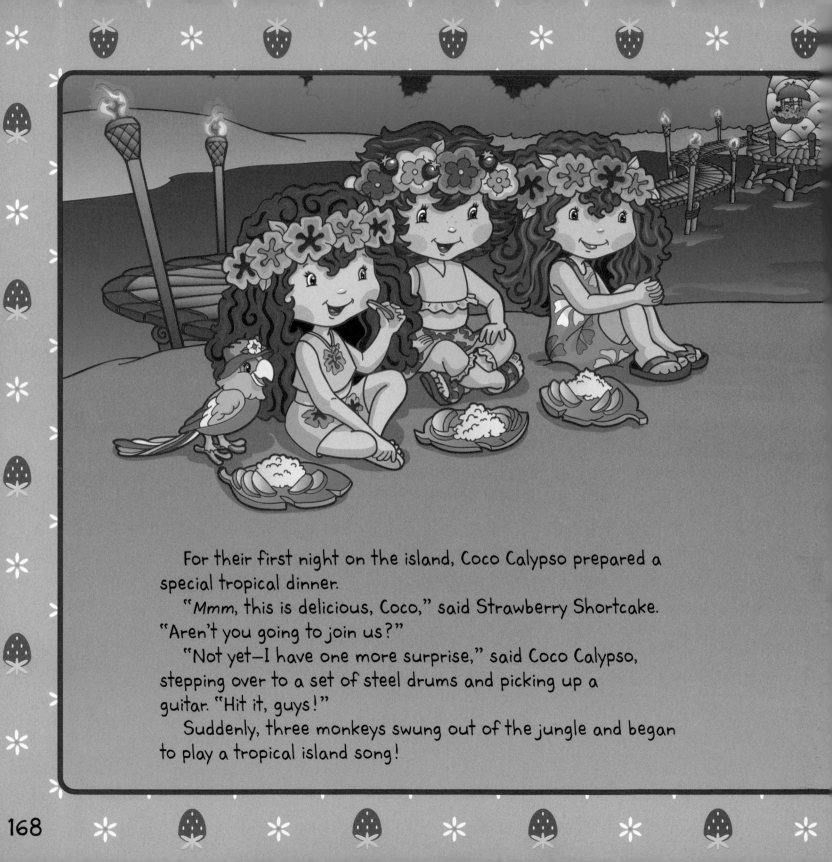

For their first night on the island, Coco Calypso prepared a special tropical dinner.

"*Mmm*, this is delicious, Coco," said Strawberry Shortcake. "Aren't you going to join us?"

"Not yet—I have one more surprise," said Coco Calypso, stepping over to a set of steel drums and picking up a guitar. "Hit it, guys!"

Suddenly, three monkeys swung out of the jungle and began to play a tropical island song!

"That was wonderful!" cried Strawberry Shortcake as Coco's song ended. "It must be berry fun to have this whole beautiful beach to yourself!"

"Oh, yeah, you bet," said Coco Calypso—but she didn't sound very convincing.

"Strawberry," whispered Blueberry Muffin. "Do you think Coco seems kind of, well, lonely?"

"I was thinking the same thing," Strawberry agreed. "Maybe that's something else we can help Coco with."

After finding a lookout spot, the girls settled in for a long watch.

"Now all we have to do is sit behind these palms and wait for—whatever it is we're waiting for," said Strawberry Shortcake.

"I'm still trying to figure out what we saw in the lagoon. Maybe it was a sea beast," Rainbow Sherbet said.

"Oh, I hope not!" exclaimed Coco Calypso. "I don't like the idea of having sea beasts in my lagoon! I hope we solve this mystery soon."

"You can count sheep on it . . . I mean, sleep on it . . . I mean, you can count on it," Strawberry yawned. "So long as we . . . don't . . . fall . . ."

The girls' eyelids grew heavier and heavier as they struggled to stay awake—but soon they were all sound asleep.

As the sun rose early the next morning, Papaya Parrot tried to crow like a rooster to wake the girls.

"Oh, no! We fell asleep!" cried Strawberry Shortcake.
"I only drifted off for a minute or two . . . or three . . .
or all night," admitted Coco.

"Look!" said Rainbow Sherbet as she pointed to the beach.
"They're gone! The seaberries are gone!" Strawberry exclaimed.

"Look!" called Blueberry Muffin as she picked up her magnifying glass. "There's a trail of seaberries leading down the beach. Follow me!"

The seaberry trail led the four friends under Coco's tropical house, around trees, and in between rocks before it finally ended right at the water's edge.

"Well, blow me over and bowl me down!" cried Rainbow Sherbet.

"This thief is a sea-thief!" added Blueberry Muffin. "And with a trail like this, it's almost like he—she—*it* wants to be caught. Maybe it really is a sea beast!"

"Oh, I'll never be able to make any more seaberry treats!" sniffled Coco Calypso as she began to cry. "And no one will ever come visit me again, not with some scary sea creature living in my lagoon. It's been so lonely here . . . and now it's going to get even lonelier."

"Don't cry, Coco—we'll solve this mystery! Let's take my boat out in the lagoon and look around," suggested Rainbow.

"Great idea!" Strawberry Shortcake said.

As Rainbow Sherbet piloted her boat out to sea, the girls searched for any sign of the sea beast.

"I don't see anything," admitted Blueberry.

"Nothing except those dark clouds on the horizon," Rainbow Sherbet said. "Could be a storm coming."

"We have to be careful. The weather changes berry fast around here," added Coco Calypso. "Check it out! Seaberries! Let's bring some back with us."

While Blueberry and Strawberry lowered the net, Rainbow and Coco secured the anchor. Soon the friends were filling basket after basket with bright, shiny seaberries.

A sudden gust of wind blew a wave aboard as a dark shadow moved over the boat.

"That storm is closer than I thought. We've got to get back to shore," warned Rainbow Sherbet. "Help me raise the anchor! Hurry!"

"Uh-oh—I think it's stuck," Strawberry Shortcake said.

"We have to pull together! Let's heave! And ho! Heave! And ho!" called Rainbow Sherbet.

The friends tugged at the anchor with all of their might, but it didn't budge.

"It's no use—the anchor is stuck!" Rainbow Sherbet yelled. "I don't know how much more my boat can take!" As the choppy sea began to rock the boat, the friends held on tight.

And then suddenly, with a *snap*, the boat started moving.

"What berry good luck!" exclaimed Strawberry Shortcake.

Rainbow Sherbet quickly pulled up the anchor line—but there was no anchor on it. "The rope's been cut!" she cried.

"That means somebody—or something—helped us," said Strawberry Shortcake.

"But who . . . and why?" asked Blueberry Muffin.

Out in the sea, a mermaid-like fin slipped into the water and disappeared.

"Look!" called Strawberry Shortcake. "Did you see that?"

"I think we all saw it," Blueberry Muffin said. "It must be the sea creature!"

"And I think we'd better get back to shore," added Rainbow Sherbet.

By the time they were back on the island, Strawberry Shortcake had come up with a plan to capture the sea creature.

"We can set a trap over here. When the thief tries to steal the seaberries, the net will pull it into the trees. The tin cans and coconuts will wake us up!"

The girls worked together to build the trap, then settled into their hiding place for the night.

Early the next morning, a loud noise woke the girls. Someone—or something—was caught in the trap!

"Be careful, Strawberry," warned Coco Calypso. "It might be dangerous."

"It might even bite," said Blueberry Muffin.

"Or claw or breathe fire or something absolutely awful!" added Rainbow Sherbet.

"Or maybe it's not a monster at all," Strawberry Shortcake said. "I'm going to let it down."

"A mermaid!" gasped Coco Calypso.

"Where? Where?" asked the thief.

"You're not a mermaid! You're a girl!" said Strawberry. "I'm Strawberry Shortcake, and these are my friends, Rainbow Sherbet, Blueberry Muffin, and Coco Calypso."

"I'm Seaberry Delight. I live in the lagoon," said Seaberry Delight.

"How'd you get my anchor?" Rainbow Sherbet asked.

"I thought you might need it back," said Seaberry Delight.

"You mean you cut the rope?" asked Strawberry.

"You looked like you were in trouble when that big storm came in. So I dove into the water and cut your anchor free. I hope you don't mind," Seaberry Delight said.

"Mind? You saved our lives! We owe you a berry big thank-you!" Strawberry said.

"If you live in the lagoon, how come I've never seen you before?" asked Coco Calypso.

"I—I'm not very good at making new friends," Seaberry Delight said shyly. "I spend most of my day growing my seaberries and feeding them to the little fish in the lagoon. But when my seaberries began disappearing, I had to do something. My friends were hungry."

"Oh, no! I thought you were stealing the seaberries from me—but I was stealing them from you!" cried Coco Calypso. "I'm berry sorry!"

"I have an idea," said Strawberry Shortcake. "Maybe Seaberry Delight can share her seaberries with Coco—and Coco can share her treats with Seaberry Delight!"

"Sounds good to me," Coco Calypso said.

"I just know the little fish will love these berrylicious treats!" Seaberry Delight replied.

"I can help Seaberry Delight grow her seaberries," Coco Calypso said.

"I can help Coco Calypso make her treats!" said Seaberry Delight.

"And you can both be the berry best of friends!" added Strawberry Shortcake—which was a berry good idea, indeed!